All Safe On Board

by Mig Holder

Illustrated by Steve Smallman

Old Noah came running across the fields in such a fluster, his coat a-flapping and his hair flying in the wind.

'Listen,' he panted to his wife. 'Listen to me!' he ordered his sons. 'Please listen,' he begged his sons' wives. 'I have been told that a great flood is coming over all our lands and we shall all be drowned!'

Noah's wife looked at him sadly. His sons looked bored. And their wives just laughed. They all went on with what they were doing.

'We need to build a huge boat,' went on Noah. 'Big enough for us and for all the animals in the forest, so that we shall be safe until the water goes away.'

Goat also went on with what he was doing, but he had been listening very carefully.

Goat talked it over with his friend, Wagtail. She put her head on one side, thinking very hard.

'But how do you know it's true?' she asked.

'I don't,' said Goat. 'But suppose it is – it would be our fault if all the animals got drowned in the flood!'

'Then we must tell them,' said Wagtail firmly. 'We must tell Snail and Dormouse and Hippo and Beaver and Owl . . .' she counted them off on her claws. '. . . and Porcupine and Giraffe and all the Monkeys and . . .'

'But they wouldn't take any notice of *me*!' said Goat.

Wagtail thought for a moment. 'We need someone important – someone they would all listen to. I know – Lion!'

'Oh no!' cried Goat, already shaking in his hooves. 'Not Lion!'

'You are funny,' laughed Wagtail. 'Why not Lion?'

'You know what Lion's like,' said Goat in a trembly voice. 'He might have me for his dinner!'

'Then we'll go together,' said Wagtail firmly, and she perched delicately on his ear.

So they set off up the hill together towards the Lion's Den, Goat dragging his hooves more and more as they went.

From the mouth of his Den, Lion saw them toiling up the hill.

'And what do you want?' he roared.

'I've come to tell you about a terrible flood that's . . . ' began Goat in a tiny, shaky voice.

'Speak up for goodness sake, Goat!' grumbled Lion.

Goat shivered and shook so much that his teeth chattered and his beard trembled.

'I . . . I . . .' But he just couldn't get the words out, he was so afraid of Lion.

'It's alright,' said Wagtail quietly. 'I'll explain.' And, completely unafraid, she flew up and whispered in Lion's great ear.

'And what does Man Noah know about anything?' sneered Lion when she had finished.

'Well, if he *is* right, and the flood comes, we'll all be drowned,' said Goat, growing braver by the minute.

Lion flicked back his mane.

'Of course, I knew that all along,' he said. Then, grandly, 'Summon the Animals!'

So the Animals were summoned.

Gradually a crowd assembled: Hippo and Beaver and the Monkeys and Porcupine and Giraffe and Owl and Elephant and . . . Dormouse.

But where was Dormouse?

When Lion thought there were enough animals to make him feel important, he tossed back his mane and cleared his throat.

'It has come to my attention,' he announced grandly, 'that a great flood is to come upon us. It will rain and rain for forty days and forty nights and all our land will be covered!'

Hippo cracked open his great jaw unexpectedly.

'How do you know this?' he asked sleepily.

For a moment Lion looked flustered. Then he sniffed, 'A little bird told me!'

'Whatever shall we do?' asked Snail in a tiny, frightened voice.

'Well, Man Noah is building some kind of a boat – an ark – that we can all go in,' explained Lion. 'But we animals must make sure he gets it right. We have our own preparations to make, and we must tell the rest of the animals in the forest. There's no time to lose!'

'Then we must hurry!' said Snail, starting to do just that.

So they all rushed off to warn every single animal in the forest about the terrible flood that was coming.

They went low . . .

. . . and high

. . . and into some *very* dangerous places.

But it's not an easy task to build a great boat. Noah was old, his wife was hot, his sons were grumpy and their wives didn't want to do it at all. And the rain was coming soon.

Behind trees and rocks and bushes, the animals watched.

'They'll never make a boat like that!' laughed Woodpecker. 'What do they know about woodwork?'

'They haven't got the first idea!' sneered the Beavers.

Goat was munching his way through a pile of leaves.

'I bet you couldn't do any better!' he said quietly, and went on chewing.

And when Noah came back after his lunch, he was amazed to see a great pile of wood, neatly stacked, ready to build the ark.

And it was like that every day.

Each time Noah and his family came back to the boat, more work seemed to have been done!

'Aren't we getting on well!' said Noah's sons, very pleased with themselves.

But Noah just looked puzzled.

And every time Noah's back was turned . . .

. . . all the animals helped.
Except the Monkeys!
And where was Dormouse?

At last it was finished.

Noah and his family stood and admired the finished ark.

'It really is a beautiful boat, Noah,' said his wife.

'We worked very hard.' said his sons.

'Can we go on board now?' asked his sons' wives.

But Noah was looking worried.

'The rain will soon be here,' he said. 'It will rain for forty days and forty nights – and then who knows how long it will be before the water drains away and we can step out onto dry land? How are we going to feed ourselves and the animals for all that time? We must get busy!'

By nightfall big piles of food had been collected and stacked and bundled and tied.

'Haven't we done well.' said Noah's sons and their wives, who actually *had* worked hard that day. 'That really must be enough.'

But Noah and his wife looked puzzled.

Had they *really* done all that work themselves?

And Goat watched thoughtfully, doing a few sums in his head.

'But why us?' asked Fennec Fox and Mole and Bat, when Goat went to call on them.

'Because we need enough supplies to last a very long time.' replied Goat, 'and there isn't much time left – the rain is on its way. The daytime animals have done their bit. You can be the night shift.'

'But nobody ever notices us,' they grumbled.

Goat slowly finished chewing his mouthful of grass.

'They might!' he said softly. 'Just see what you can do by morning.'

And he was right!

'Wow!' said Snail and Beaver and Porcupine and Giraffe next morning, when they saw the huge piles of fresh nuts and fruit and berries and leaves. 'Someone's been busy in the night!'

'That's good!' said Hippo and Rhino in chorus. 'Now we don't need to do anything.'

Goat looked up from what he was doing.

'Errm, how's all this going to get on board the boat then?' he asked mildly.

Hippo and Rhino looked first at each other and then at Goat.

'Not us!' they said. 'That's Donkey work and Horse and Ox and . . . nobody ever asks us. We don't think they *like* us.'

'They might,' replied Goat, '– if you helped.'

So they *did* help. In fact everybody helped (except the Monkeys) – even Snail, who was still hurrying.

At last all the supplies were stowed on board. Everything was ready. It was time to get on the boat.

The Animals formed a nice, tidy line.

(But where was Dormouse?)

Suddenly Monkey pulled on Camel's tail.
'Stop it!' hissed Camel, and he spat.

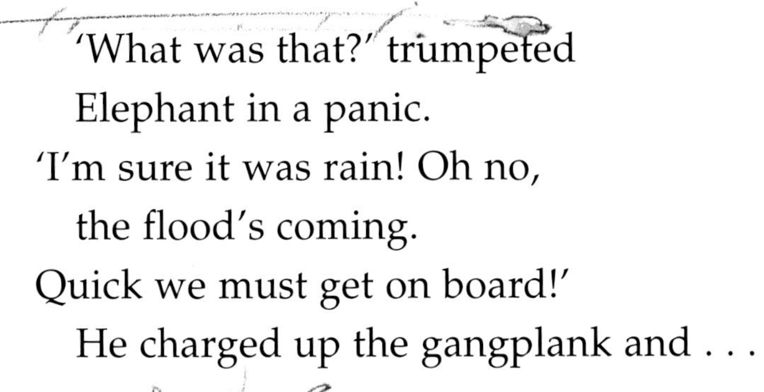

'What was that?' trumpeted Elephant in a panic.
'I'm sure it was rain! Oh no, the flood's coming.
Quick we must get on board!'
He charged up the gangplank and . . .

Crash! Splinter! Crrrrrack!
'Oh no!' cried all the animals together.
'Oh no!' cried Noah, his head in his hands.
'Poor Noah,' cried his wife and his sons
and his sons' wives.

Everybody turned to Goat.

'Goat, what shall we do now?'

Goat shook his head.

'But Goat, you always have such good ideas,' they pleaded.

'Clean out of ideas, I'm afraid,' replied Goat, chewing on a juicy piece of grass. 'You'll have to sort it out among yourselves'

And so they did.

The only problem was how to get Elephant on board.

But they soon solved that too . . . or almost.

And even Monkey helped.

Where was Dormouse?
It was time he helped.

At last everyone had clambered on board.

And the doors were firmly shut by God.

Open up this page and look inside the big boat!

'All safe on board,' said Noah. 'I did it!'

And Goat opened one sleepy eye and winked.